Timid
Tim
and the
Cuggy
Thief

For Rosalyn, Antonia and Francesca

A Red Fox Book

Published by Random House Children's Books
20 Vauxhall Bridge Road, London SW1V 2SA

A division of Random House UK Ltd
London Melbourne Sydney Auckland
Johannesburg and agencies throughout the world

Copyright © John Prater 1993

1 3 5 7 9 10 8 6 4 2

First published in Great Britain by The Bodley Head Children's Books 1993

Red Fox edition 1999

Printed in Singapore

RANDOM HOUSE UK Limited Reg. No. 954009

ISBN 0 09 9 913791-7

Timid Tim
and the
Cuggy Thief

JOHN PRATER

RED FOX

Tim was a shy little boy.

He wasn't very brave, and didn't like noisy, messy
fun or being splashed or rough and tumbles.

He didn't like big adventures.

He only wanted to be still and quiet,
with his special soft and sleepy blanket,
his cuggy. He took his cuggy
everywhere, and kept it close by
him always.

The other children would sometimes tease him by singing the CUGGY THIEF SONG!

Look out! Beware the cuggy thief
Who creeps around at night,
And steals away your favourite things
If you don't hug them tight!
They say he can be frightened off
If you put up a fight!
But none of us would ever dare
Face such an awful sight.

One dark and windy night Tim lay in bed, holding his cuggy tight.
But when he fell asleep, he tossed and turned – and let it go!

A chilling blast of air blew through the bedroom, and Tim awoke to
find his cuggy gone.

He let out a little cry, which grew bigger, and bigger, and bigger…

until he yelled at the top of his voice,
"Come back you thief! You rascal!
Give me back my cuggy!"

Tim leapt out into the night to catch the thief.

The streets were dark and empty.

The wood was darker still.

The path was steep, the mud was
deep, and though his heart beat fast,
Tim never took his eyes off the
wicked rogue ahead.

The weather grew wild, and the waves crashed loud.

But Tim bravely kept going on. He knew that he was getting close to the cuggy thief's dreadful lair.

He took a deep breath, then boldly entered the dim and rocky hole. "Give me back my cuggy," he yelled.

Tim grabbed his cuggy.
"It's mine," he shouted.
    The startled cuggy thief
grew bigger, and bigger,
and bigger, let out a
horrid scream, and
turned to pounce …

But Tim did not run. He stood quite still, and faced that awful sight.

The horrid scream grew faint until it was no more than the distant whistling of the wind. His huge darkness grew pale and thin, until it was no more than the smoke curling from the fire.

"Phew!" said Tim. "Serves you right." He knew there was nothing left of that horrid villain. The cuggy thief was gone forever.

Tim gathered together all the cuggies, teddies and best-loved toys in the wicked robber's hoard.

The boat was full for the journey home.

Everyone cheered the hero Tim for being the bravest boy ever.

But even the bravest boy ever still cuddled
cuggy for just a little longer.

Some bestselling Red Fox picture books

THE BIG ALFIE AND ANNIE ROSE STORYBOOK
by Shirley Hughes
OLD BEAR
by Jane Hissey
OI! GET OFF OUR TRAIN
by John Burningham
DON'T DO THAT!
by Tony Ross
NOT NOW, BERNARD
by David McKee
ALL JOIN IN
by Quentin Blake
THE WHALES' SONG
by Gary Blythe and Dyan Sheldon
JESUS' CHRISTMAS PARTY
by Nicholas Allan
THE PATCHWORK CAT
by Nicola Bayley and William Mayne
MATILDA
by Hilaire Belloc and Posy Simmonds
WILLY AND HUGH
by Anthony Browne
THE WINTER HEDGEHOG
by Ann and Reg Cartwright
A DARK, DARK TALE
by Ruth Brown
HARRY, THE DIRTY DOG
by Gene Zion and Margaret Bloy Graham
DR XARGLE'S BOOK OF EARTHLETS
by Jeanne Willis and Tony Ross
WHERE'S THE BABY?
by Pat Hutchins